D1165373

This book belongs to:

_____

Rockstar's Name

Rock and Roll Woods

Summary: Kuda is a bit of a grump who doesn't like change. So when he wakes up to find new neighbors and loud, strange noises in his woods, he is not happy. Will his desire to be with his friends overcome his objections to loud sounds? And might Kuda's courage help him discover that new things and rock and roll music can be pretty great? Featuring helpful backmatter about Sensory Integration and insider jokes for parents with autistic kids.

Clear Fork Publishing P.O. Box 870 102 S. Swenson Stamford, Texas 79553 (325)773-5550 **clearforkpublishing.com** Spork Children's Books. Hand lettering by Anika A. Wolf. The fonts used in this book are: Baskerville OldFace and Calibri.

Printed and Bound in the United States of America.

ISBN - 978-1-946101-68-6
LCN - 2018947251

ROCK &ROLL WOODS

Written by Sherry Howard
Illustrated by Anika A. Wolf

Kuda woke up from a beary long sleep. He loved the soft sounds of his neighborhood.

Whoosh! Whoosh! Whoosh! The stream gurgled.

Chirrup! Chirrup! Chirrup! The birds chirped.

Swish! Swish! Swish! The forest floor rustled.

BOOM whappa whappa

BOOM whappa whappa

Kuda set off on his daily walk.

What was that? He clamped his paws over his ears. *What was that AWFUL noise?*

"What's the racket?" Kuda asked.
Rabbit's foot thumpity thumped to
the beat.

"We have new neighbors."

Kuda groaned, "New loud noises and new neighbors."

BOOM whappa whappa
BOOM whappa whappa
BOOM BOOM BOOM

"I don't like it," grumbled Kuda.
"It's too loud."

"You'll feel better after you eat."
Rabbit led Kuda to the water.

While Kuda ate, Rabbit bounced to the rhythm of the music. Kuda had never seen him so happy, hopping all around.

Kuda almost swished his behind along to the tune, but then he remembered he didn't like new noises.

"What do *you* think of the new racket?" Kuda asked. Surely, Owl didn't like these new sounds.

"WHO? Me?" Owl's head bobbed again on a

BOOM
BOOM
BOOM

Squirrel scampered past, shaking his bushy tail to the beat. "Come on! Join the fun."

"I don't like it," grumbled Kuda. "It's too loud. I can't hear the stream, or the birds, or even think."

Kuda tramped back to his cave leaving Rabbit confused.

"How can anyone not like the music?" Rabbit wondered.

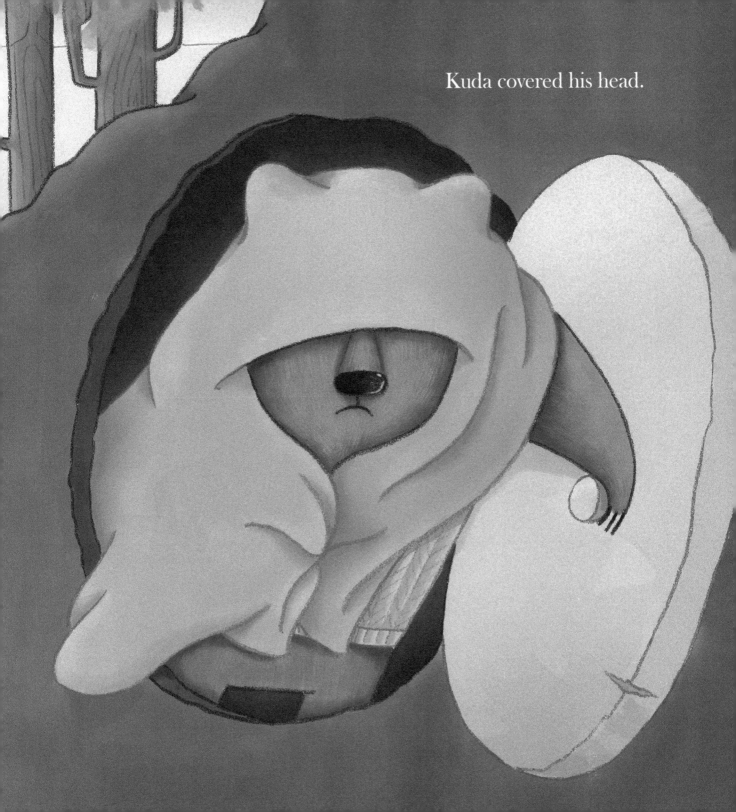

Kuda covered his head.

Kuda found his earmuffs and scarf.

BOOM whappa whappa whappa

Then he added layers. . .

and layers. . .

and more layers.

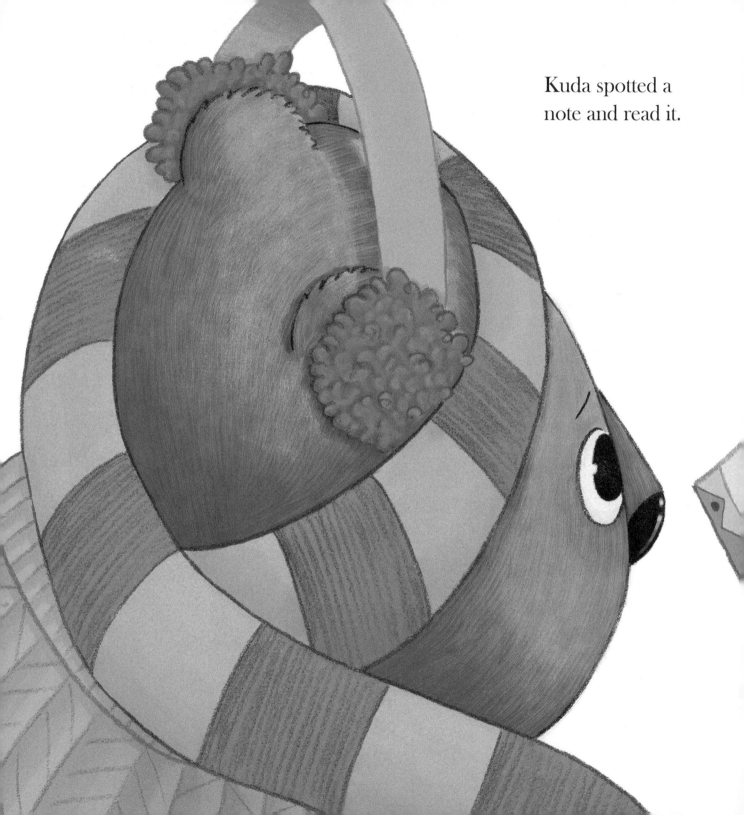

Kuda spotted a
note and read it.

Please join our

ROCK & ROLL celebration

in the community cabin

He sniffled. Tired of being alone, Kuda headed off to see what all the fuss was about.

whappa whappa

As Kuda got closer and closer, the music got louder and louder. He peeked inside...

And that's when he saw his friends dancing to the...

They swirled and twirled,
dipped and dropped,
clapped and stomped.

Kuda felt the sounds thumping in his chest—

BO•M
BO•M
BO•M

He felt his paws pick up sticks and beat time on a fallen log.

BO•M whappa whappa

It was as if his body had a mind of its own.

Strange, his ears didn't hurt so much.

Maybe the new noise wasn't so bad. That drum
looked more fun than sticks on a log.

Kuda wanted to be with his friends. Maybe he'd
go in . . . just for a few minutes.

Community
cabin
WELCOME

When Kuda finally opened the door, his friends cheered!

"Was that you on the wood outside?" the new neighbor asked.
She motioned Kuda to sit at the drums and pound a beat.

Kuda quickly found his rhythm.

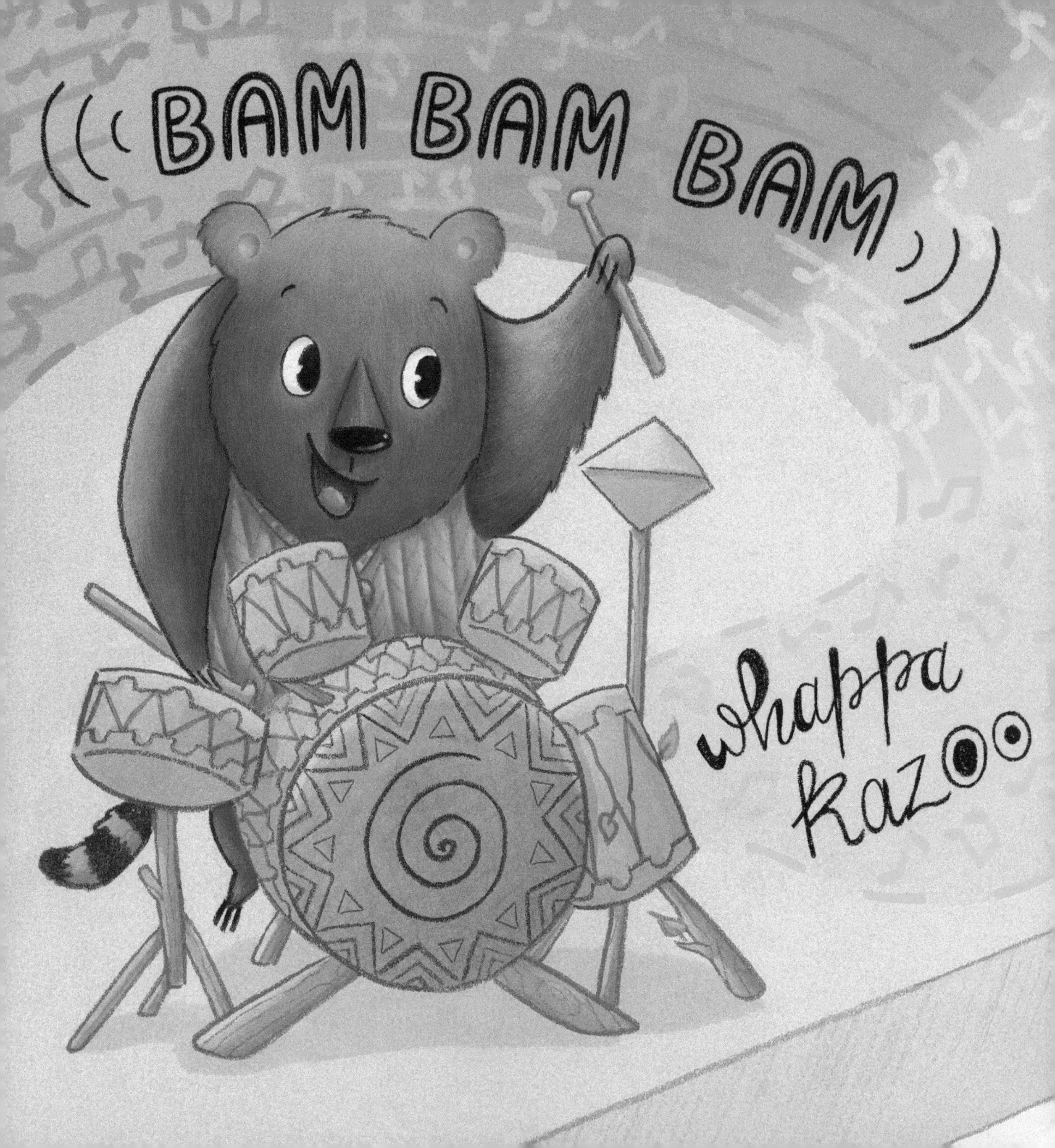
BAM BAM BAM
whappa
kazoo

Owl chimed in. Who, who, who.

Rabbit thumpity thumped.

Old and new friends jammed together.

After the party ended Kuda ambled back to his cave. Rabbit hopped alongside him.

"Wasn't that fun? You learned the drums."

Kuda hated to admit that he liked the new noises in his woods.

"It was okay."

"Our new neighbors are so fun," Rabbit
said. "I can't wait until the next party."

"They're okay," said Kuda. "Guess I could
get used to a rock and roll woods."

Swish! Swish! Swish! The forest floor
rustled as the old friends returned home.

Author's Note

When I wrote Rock and Roll Woods, I imagined a story that all children would love. What young child wouldn't love a bear named Kuda? So, one layer of this story is about a grumpy bear learning to try new things. By trying new things, Kuda finds his love for rock and roll music, especially the drums.

I also wanted another layer for some special people—those children who process things a little differently. I used what I'd learned as a parent, teacher, advocate, and administrator to inspire children with sensory integration issues.

So, what are sensory integration problems? They are a lot of different things.

A loud clap of thunder nearby makes almost anybody jump. But, what if a small bouncing ball sounded like thunder? Or, what if a tag in the collar of your shirt felt like a raccoon gnawing on your neck? That's how some children process sounds and touch.

Did you notice how Kuda didn't like new things or loud noises at first? There are kids just like Kuda. They might be kids who just don't like loud music. But they might be kids who have sensory integration problems, or they might have something called autism.

Children with sensory processing issues process the world around them in a different way. It's different for each of them, just as each snowflake is unique.

Sensory Integration

Some sensory integration issues might be:

- fear of loud noises

- dislike of being touched by other people

- dislike of texture in food or clothes

- love of repetition, doing the same thing over and over

- avoidance of new activities, love of routine

- stronger reactions than expected in the situation

Let's all help our friends who see and hear things a little differently. Be a good friend like Rabbit and Squirrel and Owl were to Kuda. Be patient.

I hope Kuda's bravery to try something new will inspire kids to channel their own courage.

With lots of love to all my readers and their parents,

Sherry Howard, M. Ed.,
KY CEC Outstanding Special Education Administrator

SHERRY HOWARD lives with her children and dogs in Middletown, Kentucky. She was an educator who loved working with all children, but children with special needs stole her heart. Sherry has fond memories of her husband's rock and roll band, but sadly, she never got past strumming a ukulele herself. Visit her at sherryhoward.org

Rock and Roll Woods is Sherry's debut picture book.

ANIKA A. WOLF loves telling stories through illustration, writing and graphic design. She hates to admit this, but she *likes* singing at the top of her lungs (but only when she's by herself). If she were in a rock and roll band, her instrument of choice would be the banjo. Visit her online at anikawolf.com

Rock and Roll Woods is Anika's debut picture book.

Many thanks to: My beloved parents for raising readers.
My grands for listening, especially Kamora for imagining Kuda into creation.
All the children who fear new things . . . may this help you find your courage. Be strong! — S.H.

For my Miss, who now has a little rockstar of her own — A.A.W.

CPSIA information can be obtained
at www.ICGtesting.com
Printed in the USA
LVHW071543200119
604582LV00019B/395/P